PREVIOUS PAGE: THESE TOWERS OF INTERSTELLAR DUST AND GAS ARE CALLED THE PILLARS OF CREATION. THEY CAN BE FOUND ABOUT 7,000 LIGHT-YEARS FROM EARTH, IN THE EAGLE NEBULA. THIS AWESOME IMAGE WAS TAKEN IN 1995 BY THE HUBBLE SPACE TELESCOPE.

NATIONAL GEOGRAPHIC
KiDS

CAN'T GET
ENOUGH

SPACE
Stuff

FUN FACTS,
AWESOME
INFO, COOL
GAMES,
SILLY JOKES,
AND MORE!

JULIE BEER AND
STEPHANIE WARREN DRIMMER

NATIONAL GEOGRAPHIC
WASHINGTON, D.C.

TABLE OF CONTENTS

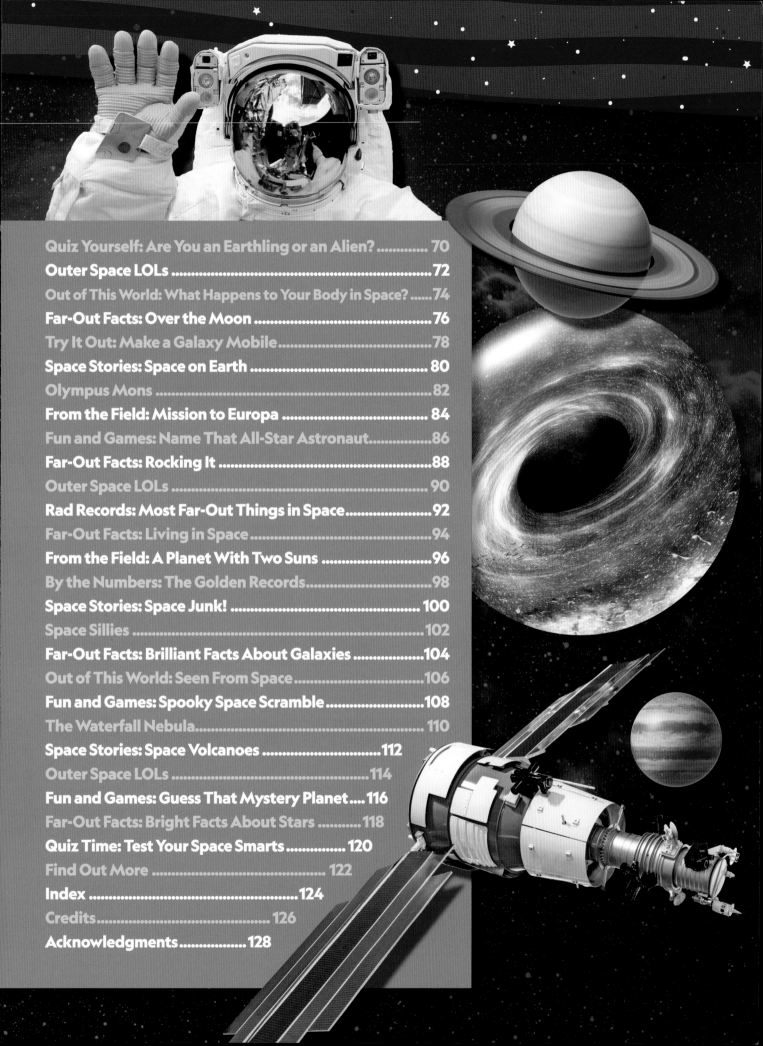

3-2-1... BLAST OFF!

FOR HUNDREDS OF YEARS, astronomers have turned their telescopes to the night sky, discovering everything from comets to black holes to planetary rings made of ice and rock. So far, Earth is the only planet we know of that supports life, but scientists continue to scan our galaxy and others for the possibility of extraterrestrials. But humans aren't content to just study space from Earth: A group of astronauts live on board the International Space Station, orbiting some 250 miles (400 km) above Earth, and someday in the not too distant future, humans may set up a colony on Mars.

This book is your source for supersize space fun. Inside, you can explore space facts, take quizzes to test your space smarts, and giggle at some galactic jokes. Get the scoop on space food, space junk, and space volcanoes. Learn about how scientists are looking for life on other planets, the ins and outs of our solar system, mind-blowing black holes, what happens to your body in space, and much, much more.

So, get ready: It's time to explore moons, planets, stars, and beyond!

ILLUSTRATION OF SPACEX'S CREW DRAGON AND FALCON 9 ROCKET

GALACTIC GLOSSARY

How well do you know your space language? Test your knowledge by matching each term with its definition. Grab a word (numbers) and see if you can match it with the correct definition (letters). Write your answers on a separate piece of paper. Then compare them to the answer key on the side of page 9.

1	2	3	4
GRAVITY	**NASA**	**MASS**	**G-FORCE**

5	6	7	8
LIGHT-YEAR	**ATMOSPHERE**	**INTERSTELLAR**	**EXOPLANET**

9	10	11	12
GALAXY	**QUASAR**	**COMET**	**METEOR**

13	14	15	16
METEORITE	**ASTEROID**	**NEBULA**	**STAR**

17	18	19	20
CONSTELLATION	**BLACK HOLE**	**SUPERNOVA**	**ROVER**

A The distance light travels in one year, roughly six trillion miles (10 trillion km)	**B** A vehicle that explores the surface of a moon or a planet	**C** The part of space that exists between the stars	**D** The amount of matter or substance that makes up an object
E A huge collection of gas, dust, and billions of stars and their planets, all held together by gravity	**F** The space exploration organization of the United States; short for National Aeronautics and Space Administration	**G** The force of gravity pulling on an object	**H** A planet outside our solar system
I A pulling force that exists across space and between objects	**J** An extremely bright faraway object in space that gives off large amounts of energy	**K** A small, rocky body that orbits the sun; sometimes called a planetoid or minor planet	**L** A "dirty snowball" of frozen gases, rock, and dust
M A place in space where the gravitational pull is so strong not even light can escape it	**N** A giant cloud of gas and dust	**O** The mixture of gases that surrounds a planet	**P** A meteoroid that has survived its trip through Earth's atmosphere and landed on Earth's surface
Q A group of stars that forms a shape when the "dots" are connected	**R** The explosion of a massive star	**S** A space rock (meteoroid) that has entered Earth's atmosphere	**T** A big ball of gas that gives off heat and light

ANSWERS: 1. I, 2. F, 3. D, 4. G, 5. A, 6. O, 7. C, 8. H, 9. E, 10. J 11. L, 12. S, 13. P, 14. K, 15. N, 16. T, 17. Q, 18. M, 19. R, 20. B

LOOKING FOR LIFE

SCIENTISTS ARE SEARCHING OUTER SPACE FOR "TECHNOSIGNATURES"— RADIO OR LASER SIGNALS, A SIGN OF INTELLIGENT LIFE.

SCIENTISTS ARE SEARCHING FOR LIFE ON OTHER PLANETS.

How will they know if they've found it? To date, Earth is the only place in the universe we know of that supports life. What makes the Earth able to support living things?

WATER IS LIFE

For starters, Earth has liquid water, which was key to the beginning of life here. All living things on our planet need water to survive, and Earth is the only planet in our solar system with large oceans on its surface. It's also in the solar system's sweet spot: It's not too close to the sun so it doesn't get too hot, and not too far away so it's not super cold.

OUR GALACTIC NEIGHBORS

Scientists have found more than 3,200 solar systems in our galaxy ... and they estimate there may be tens of billions! Scientists are looking at them to see if they have planets similar to Earth

THE ONLY LIFE THAT EXISTED ON EARTH FOR ROUGHLY ITS FIRST FOUR BILLION YEARS WERE TINY ONE-CELLED MICROBES.

that might sustain life. They're especially interested in finding planets that have oxygen and methane—gases released into the air by living things. Many of these planets are so far away that with today's technology we can't get a good look at them. But as technology improves, we'll learn more about them.

ASTEROIDS AND COMETS
Asteroids and comets orbit stars just as planets do. Could they support life? Scientists think it's possible. But the hunt for life in our solar system and beyond won't necessarily reveal the exact sort of intelligent life found on Earth. What scientists hope to find are beings that learn and understand, and possibly can send communication, signaling to let us know they're there. Scientists recently estimated that there are only a few dozen planets in our galaxy capable of supporting such life.

SPACE SILLIES

KNOCK, KNOCK.

Who's there?
Solar.
Solar who?
Solar you going to laugh at my joke?

Q What is an astronaut's favorite key on a computer keyboard?

A The space bar!

Q Why did the constellation Leo get into trouble?

A It was lion.

TONGUE TWISTER

SAY THIS FAST THREE TIMES:
Marcia moved to Mars to meet a Martian.

Q What type of music do planets listen to?

Q Why did the sun go to school?

A To get brighter!

A Nep-tunes!

RIDDLE ME THIS ...

Q Which is lighter, the sun or Earth?

A The sun, because it rises every morning.

P PARKING

EFRATA: Where do astronauts park their spaceships?

MIGUEL: Next to the space station?

EFRATA: No, next to a parking meteor!

IS THERE ANYONE OUT THERE?

ASTRONOMERS HAVE DISCOVERED MORE THAN 4,000 PLANETS OUTSIDE OUR SOLAR SYSTEM. THESE ARE KNOWN AS EXOPLANETS.

Since all life on Earth needs liquid water to survive, many astronomers are **ON THE HUNT FOR OCEAN WORLDS** other than our own.

Our galaxy, the Milky Way, contains at least 100 billion planets.

There are more than 2,000,000,000,000 (two trillion!) galaxies in the universe.

When the alien-hunting **Extremely Large Telescope** is completed, it will be **more powerful** than all the other large telescopes in the world **combined.**

Scientists at the SETI Institute scan the sky for signals from alien life, such as strange radio signals or flashing lasers.

About 3.5 billion years ago, **Mars also had rivers and lakes,** like Earth.

Experts think the EXOPLANET KEPLER 425 B, 1,400 light-years from Earth, HAS A THICK ATMOSPHERE, LIQUID WATER, and volcanoes—perhaps PERFECT CONDITIONS FOR LIFE.

Jupiter's moon Europa has a salty ocean beneath its icy surface that could be home to life-forms.

Some experts think we'll find evidence of life beyond Earth within the next few decades.

MOST PECULIAR PLANETS

BLINGIEST PLANET

55 CANCRI E

In 2004, scientists discovered a strange new type of planet orbiting a nearby star in the Milky Way galaxy. Experts believe at least a third of the planet is made of pure diamond. Experts estimate its value at about $26.9 nonillion (26.9 followed by 29 zeros).

WORST WEATHER

COROT-7 B

On Earth, rain can be unpleasant. On planet CoRoT-7 b, it can be downright deadly. Instead of a water cycle, scientists think this planet has a rock cycle: Liquid rock on its surface rises and forms clouds that rain down pebbles.

GRANDPA PLANET

PSR B1620-26 B

Scientists got a shock when they calculated the age of PSR B1620-26 b, a planet near the edge of the Milky Way galaxy. It's about 13 billion years old, making it more than twice as old as Earth and the oldest planet ever found.

WETTEST PLANET

GJ 1214 B

GJ 1214b is a "super Earth" about six times more massive than our planet. It's also likely to be surrounded by a thick, steamy atmosphere made of water.

GAS GIANT

HAT-P-67 B

The largest planet known, HAT-P-67 b, is more than twice as wide as Jupiter, making it nearly 200,000 miles (322,000 km) across. This mega-planet is so close to its star that it takes only 4.8 Earth days to complete an orbit.

OUR SOLAR SYSTEM

Our solar system, located in the Milky Way galaxy, consists of one star (the sun), eight planets (Mercury, Venus, Earth, Mars, Jupiter, Saturn, Uranus, and Neptune), several dwarf planets (including Pluto), hundreds of moons, and millions of asteroids, comets, and meteoroids.

THE SUN

Age: 4.5 billion years

Average surface temperature: 10,300°F (5700°C)

Light: It takes eight minutes and 20 seconds for the light leaving the sun to reach Earth.

MARS

Location: Fourth planet from the sun

Distance from sun: 128,409,598 to 154,865,853 miles (206,669,000 to 249,209,300 km)

Average surface temperature: Minus 20°F (-28°C)

EARTH

Location: Third planet from the sun

Distance from sun: 91,402,640 to 94,509,460 miles (147,098,291 to 152,098,233 km)

Average surface temperature: 61°F (16°C)

VENUS

Location: Second planet from the sun

Distance from sun: 66,782,596 to 67,693,905 miles (107,477,000 to 108,939,000 km)

Average surface temperature: 880°F (471°C)

MERCURY

Location: First planet from the sun

Distance from sun: 28,583,702 to 35,983,125 miles (46,001,200 to 69,816,900 km)

Average surface temperature: 800°F (430°C) during the day, minus 290°F (-180°C) at night

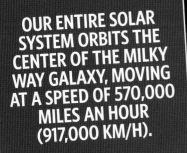

OUR ENTIRE SOLAR SYSTEM ORBITS THE CENTER OF THE MILKY WAY GALAXY, MOVING AT A SPEED OF 570,000 MILES AN HOUR (917,000 KM/H).

JUPITER

Location: Fifth planet from the sun

Distance from sun: 460,237,112 to 507,040,015 miles (740,679,835 to 816,001,807 km)

Average surface temperature: Minus 162°F (-108°C)

SATURN

Location: Sixth planet from the sun

Distance from sun: 838,741,509 to 934,237,322 miles (1,349,823,615 to 1,503,509,229 km)

Average surface temperature: Minus 218°F (-138°C)

URANUS

Location: Seventh planet from the sun

Distance from sun: 1,699,449,110 to 1,868,039,489 miles (2,734,998,229 to 3,006,318,143 km)

Average surface temperature: Minus 320°F (-195°C)

ASTEROID BELT

Contents: Rubble left over from the solar system's formation

Location: A stretch of space between Mars and Jupiter

Size: Asteroids range in size from dwarf planets nearly 600 miles (950 km) across to rocks less than half a mile (1 km) wide.

NEPTUNE

Location: Eighth planet from the sun

Distance from sun: 2,771,162,074 to 2,819,185,846 miles (4,459,753,056 to 4,537,039,826 km)

Average surface temperature: Minus 331°F (-201°C)

MARS IS TRULY OUT OF THIS WORLD

If you were to pour out a glass of water on Mars, it would **INSTANTLY BOIL AND DISAPPEAR.**

Mars has two moons, **Phobos and Deimos.**

Mars has less gravity than Earth. A kid weighing 60 pounds (27 kg) here would weigh about 23 pounds (11 kg) on Mars.

Someday, Mars may have rings like Saturn's. That could happen millions of years from now, when its moon Phobos breaks up and the pieces surround the planet.

IT HASN'T RAINED ON MARS
in millions of years.

The red planet appears orange-red in the night sky because its **surface contains a lot of iron oxide**—also known as **rust.**

On Earth, you can jump about 1.6 feet (0.5 m) into the air. On Mars, **you could spring about three feet (0.9 m) off the surface**—and stay in the air for two seconds!

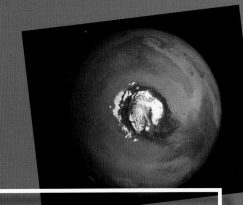

Enormous dust storms
sometimes cover the entire red planet.

In 2018, scientists discovered **EVIDENCE OF A LAKE OF LIQUID WATER** located a mile (1.6 km) beneath Mars's south pole. Since then, they've found even more lakes.

WHICH PLANET ARE YOU?

IF THESE DESCRIPTIONS DON'T FIT YOU, THAT'S OK. THIS QUIZ IS JUST FOR FUN!

Planets are unique, and so are people. Take this quiz to find out which of these planets you are most like.

What's your ideal vacation?

a. a camel ride in the Sahara desert

b. climbing to the top of Mount Everest

c. sightseeing in a big city like Tokyo

d. a weekend at a luxury hotel, the fancier the better

e. an expedition to Antarctica, the southernmost place on the globe

Friends would describe you as _____.

a. fiery—you're a little hotheaded at times

b. outdoorsy—you'd rather be hiking

c. social—you like to be surrounded by others

d. creative—you think outside the box

e. quiet—you can be a little shy

What would you want as a superpower?

a. the ability to throw fireballs

b. the ability to summon storms

c. super strength

d. a magic lasso

e. the ability to turn objects into ice

What's your favorite after-school activity?

a. doing some gardening

b. climbing to the top of the jungle gym at the park

c. joining friends for a game of soccer

d. doing a craft project—the more glitter the better

e. sitting under a tree and reading a good book

What's your fashion style?

a. unique—you don't feel the need to dress like everyone else

b. warm colors, like reds and oranges

c. stripes and patterns

d. the more bling the better

e. cool colors, like blues and violet

ADD UP YOUR SCORE!
a=1 b=2 c=3 d=4 e=5

5-9 Points
You are most like Venus.
You can take the heat, and you like to keep things simple. Venus is the second closest planet to the sun, but it has the hottest temperatures. It's also special—it spins the opposite direction of Earth and most other planets, and its rotation is very slow.

10-14 Points
You are most like Mars.
You have a sense of adventure. Also known as the red planet, Mars is rocky and sometimes has massive dust storms. Robots have been exploring this planet since 1997.

15-19 Points
You are most like Jupiter.
You like to be where the action is. Jupiter is the largest planet in the solar system—it's twice as massive as all the other planets in the solar system combined. This planet is also a gas giant—it's not solid like Earth. Its stripes come from swirling clouds, and it has 79 moons to keep it company.

20-24 Points
You are most like Saturn.
You're creative and don't mind standing out in a crowd. Saturn is most famous for its stunning rings—made up of millions of pieces of ice and rock. But rings aren't its only accessory: Saturn also has 53 named moons and at least 29 more waiting to be confirmed.

25-29 Points
You are most like Neptune.
You're a quiet observer who avoids being the center of attention. Neptune is the farthest planet from the sun, which means it's chilly: The average temperature is minus 331°F (-201°C). It also has powerful winds that are five times stronger than the strongest winds recorded on Earth.

OUTER SPACE LOLs

KNOCK, KNOCK.

Who's there?
Solar.
Solar who?
Solar you coming out for a space walk, or what?

Q How do you know when the moon has had plenty to eat?

A When it's full.

Q What do astronauts on the International Space Station do when they get cold?

A They turn on a space heater.

RIDDLE ME THIS ...

Q What hangs around at night but goes away during the day?

A The moon.

HAILEY: Where do astronauts keep their sandwiches?

TONY: Where?

HAILEY: Their launch boxes!

JADEN: Where do Martians put their teacups?

ELIJAH: I don't know. Where?

JADEN: On flying saucers.

Q How do you get a baby astronaut to stop crying?

A You rocket.

BLACK HOLE COLLISION

THE MILKY WAY HAS A HUGE BLACK HOLE AT ITS CENTER CALLED SAGITTARIUS A* (A-STAR).

In 2019, astronomers peering skyward discovered something unexpected: three supersize black holes on a collision course. They're located a billion light-years from Earth, in three faraway galaxies.

A BLACK HOLE IS BORN

Most of the time, a black hole is born when a large star dies. If a star is big enough, it explodes in what's called a supernova. It flings matter out into space, leaving behind just its heavy core. The core's gravity is so strong that it begins to collapse. And it doesn't stop. It becomes a tiny point with extremely powerful gravity: a black hole. Some black holes can have the gravity of 10 suns packed into a spot the size of New York City. The gravity of a black hole is so strong that nothing can escape, not even light. This makes a black hole look like an empty place in space.

SCIENTISTS SNAPPED THE FIRST EVER PICTURE OF A BLACK HOLE IN 2019.

SPACE JAM

Scientists think that giant black holes may be at the center of every large galaxy. If galaxies crash into each other as they move through space, their black holes can merge to form even bigger black holes. But this process could take one billion years! Astronomers will have to be patient to see what happens when the three newly discovered black holes meet.

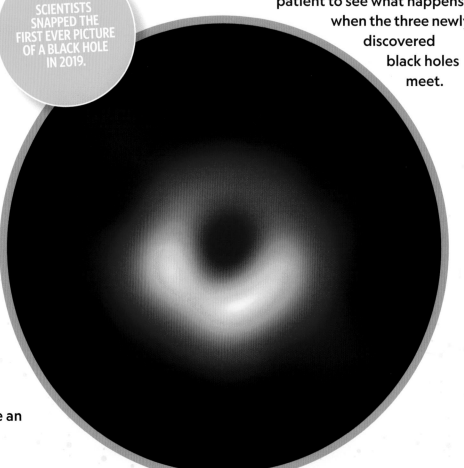

A BLACK HOLE CAN CONTINUE TO GROW THROUGHOUT ITS LIFE.

WITH AN AVERAGE TEMPERATURE OF

MORE THAN 850°F (454°C),

VENUS IS THE

HOTTEST PLANET

IN THE SOLAR SYSTEM.

ILLUSTRATION
SHOWING THE
ROCKY SURFACE
OF VENUS

VENUS'S **HIGH TEMPERATURE** DOESN'T COME FROM ITS LOCATION—MERCURY IS ACTUALLY CLOSER TO THE SUN. INSTEAD, **VENUS HAS THICK CLOUDS THAT ACT LIKE A BLANKET.**

HOW LONG IS A DAY?

On Earth, a day is 24 hours—about how long it takes our planet to make one full rotation on its axis. But other planets spin at different speeds. If you spent a day on another planet in our solar system, it would either fly by or seem like an eternity, depending on where you were.

= 24 HOURS

Neptune
1 NEPTUNE DAY: 16 hours

Saturn
1 SATURN DAY: 11 hours

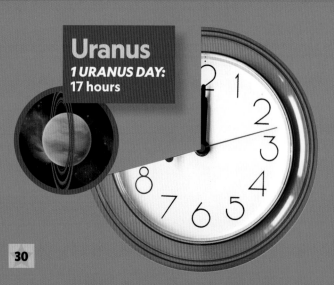

Uranus
1 URANUS DAY: 17 hours

Jupiter
1 JUPITER DAY: 10 hours

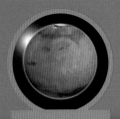

Mars
1 MARS DAY:
25 hours

Earth
1 EARTH DAY:
24 hours

Venus
1 VENUS DAY:
5,832 hours

Mercury
1 MERCURY DAY:
1,408 hours

A ROTATION IS A PLANET'S SPINNING MOTION AROUND ITS OWN AXIS. A REVOLUTION IS ITS MOVEMENT AROUND ANOTHER OBJECT (LIKE THE SUN).

OUR AMAZING SOLAR SYSTEM

More than **one million Earths** could fit inside the sun.

OUR SOLAR SYSTEM HAS FIVE KNOWN DWARF PLANETS: CERES, PLUTO, HAUMEA, MAKEMAKE, AND ERIS.

Winds on Venus can reach about **250 miles an hour** (400 km/h).

MORE THAN 99 PERCENT OF THE SOLAR SYSTEM'S MASS COMES FROM THE SUN. (MASS IS THE AMOUNT OF MATTER THERE IS IN SOMETHING.)

Uranus rotates sideways.

SUNSETS ON MARS **LOOK BLUE.**

Mercury is shrinking. It's about 8.6 miles (14 km) smaller in diameter than it was about four billion years ago.

JUPITER'S MOON IO HAS MORE THAN 400 ACTIVE VOLCANOES, making it the most volcanically active world in the solar system.

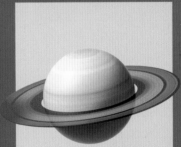

Saturn's rings span about 175,000 miles (282,000 km).

An asteroid called Chariklo has rings.

Earth's **days** are getting **longer.**

Pluto is **half as wide** as the United States.

Rocks from Mars have crashed to Earth.

Venus's surface is **SO HOT** it could **MELT TIN AND LEAD.**

There are more than 200 moons in our solar system.

The **biggest moon** in the solar system is Ganymede, a moon of Jupiter that is larger than the planet Mercury.

Our entire solar system orbits the center of the Milky Way. One orbit takes about 230 million years.

Jupiter's giant red spot

JUPITER'S GIANT RED SPOT IS A SWIRLING STORM WIDER THAN EARTH.

THE SPACE PLACE

THE ISS TRAVELS AT 17,500 MILES AN HOUR (28,000 KM/H).

About 250 miles (400 km) above Earth's surface floats the most unusual human dwelling in the known universe: the incredible International Space Station, or ISS. This orbiting science laboratory has been home to a rotating crew of astronauts since 2000.

HOME AWAY FROM HOME

The International Space Station gets its power from solar panels and its supplies from U.S. and Russian resupply missions. Astronauts usually spend about six months at a time aboard the ISS, doing science experiments and keeping the spacecraft in working condition. Sometimes, their missions last much longer: NASA astronaut Scott Kelly spent a year on the ISS, from March 27, 2015, to March 2, 2016. The goal was to help scientists better

understand how the human body would be able to handle long space missions, such as a future trip to Mars.

BIG BUILD

The ISS took 13 years to construct. It was sent to space in pieces and put together in orbit. Today, it's a floating workspace and residence bigger than a six-bedroom house! It has sleeping quarters for six people, plus two bathrooms, a gym, and a bay window with a pretty spectacular view!

THE ISS WAS SENT TO SPACE IN PIECES AND CONSTRUCTED IN ORBIT.

SPACE SILLIES

RIDDLE ME THIS ...

Q What planet has art inside it?

A eARTh!

Q How do you organize a space-themed party?

A You plan-et!

Q If athletes get athlete's foot, what do astronauts get?

A Missile-toe.

TONGUE TWISTER

SAY THIS FAST THREE TIMES:
Spaceships swiftly steer through space at light speed.

YOU'VE GOT TO BE JOKING ...

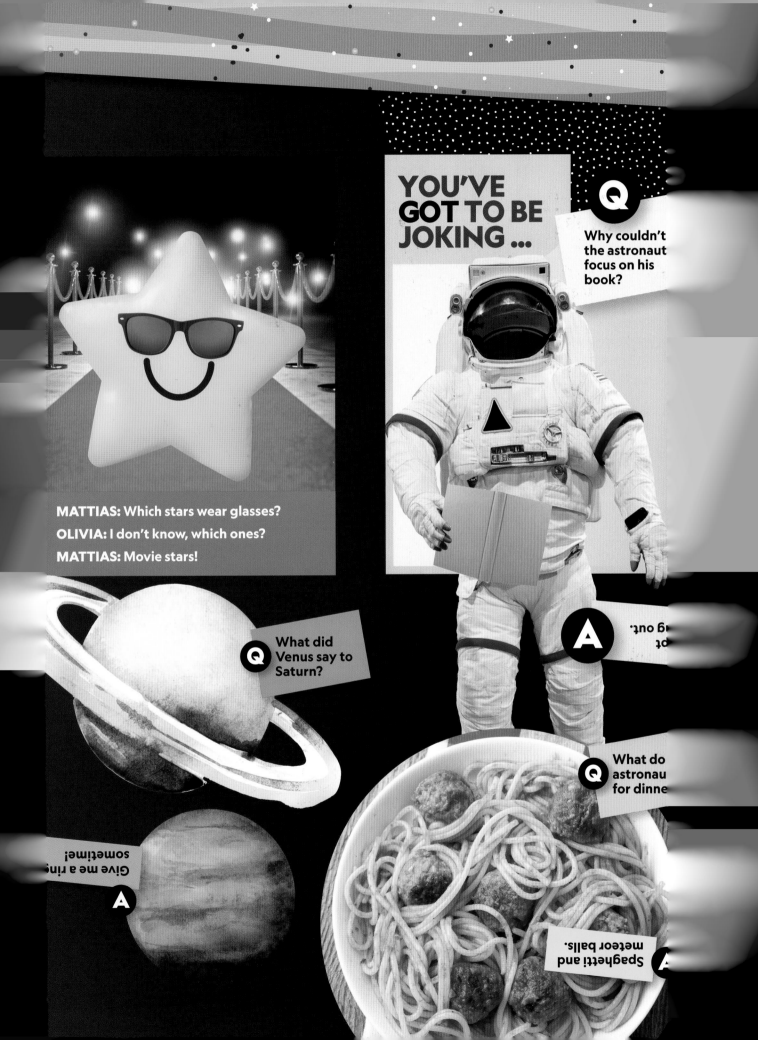

MATTIAS: Which stars wear glasses?
OLIVIA: I don't know, which ones?
MATTIAS: Movie stars!

Q Why couldn't the astronaut focus on his book?

A ...g out.

Q What did Venus say to Saturn?

A Give me a ring sometime!

Q What do astronau for dinne

A Spaghetti and meteor balls.

LOST IN SPACE

The Moon Rock concert just ended, but now these aliens can't find their spaceships in the parking lot. To help each alien locate its spaceship, follow these rules, then check your answers in the answer key on the side of the page.

Aliens with antennae need ships with pointed roofs.	Short aliens need ladders to reach the doors of their ships.
Purple aliens must return to the Purple Planet in purple spaceships.	The number of windows on the spaceship must match the number of eyeballs on the alien.

THANKS for COMING!

MOON-ROCK-A-THON!

EXIT

Galaxy's Child
Moon tour 2004

space

THE ASTRONAUT FOOTPRINTS

ON THE MOON COULD BE THERE FOR

A MILLION YEARS.

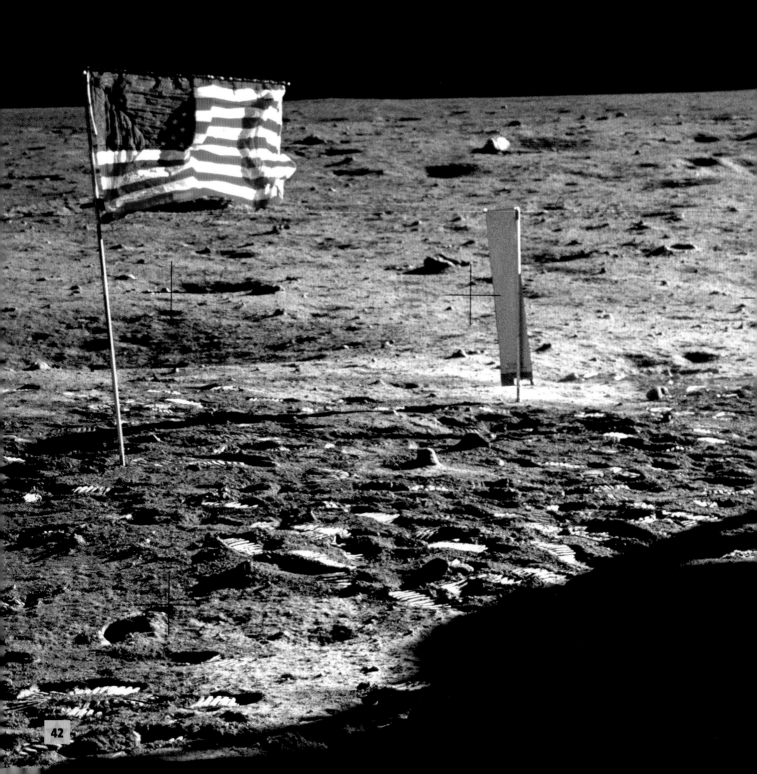

BECAUSE THE MOON HAS NO ATMOSPHERE, THERE IS NO WIND TO BLOW THE DUST AND ERASE THE FOOTPRINTS.

MOVING TO MARS

IT WOULD TAKE ASTRONAUTS ABOUT SIX MONTHS TO REACH MARS.

FOR DECADES, HUMANS HAVE IMAGINED NOT ONLY EXPLORING THE RED PLANET, but also sending people to live there for long periods of time. Scientists think it is possible, but not without overcoming a whole lot of obstacles.

GETTING COMFORTABLE

For starters, Mars has a thin atmosphere that is mostly carbon dioxide and doesn't have breathable oxygen. You could bring oxygen to Mars from Earth, but that would be expensive and bulky. So NASA scientists have invented a device that converts carbon dioxide into oxygen. People living on Mars would have to wear special space suits that would give them oxygen and keep their body temperature at a comfortable level. Buildings on Mars would need to be constructed, likely using 3D printers and Mars's red sand as a building material. They would be partially underground to help protect against the planet's average subzero temperatures.

GROWING FOOD

Another not-so-small problem: There's no food or water on the surface of the planet. Satellite radars could be used to try to find stores of underground ice that could be tapped for water. And settlers would need to start making their own food. Scientists think crops like beans, peas, and asparagus would grow well in soil there, which means the first settlers would have to add farming to their list of skills!

OUTER SPACE LOLs

KNOCK, KNOCK.

Who's there?
Alien.
Alien who?
What do you mean "who"? How many aliens do you know?!

Q What's an astronaut's favorite music?

A Rocket and roll.

Q What do you call the first day of the week in space?

Sun	Mon	Tue	Wed	Thu	Fri	Sat
1	2	3	4	5	6	7
8	9	10	11	12	13	14
15	16	17	18	19	20	21
22	23	24	25	26	27	28
29	30	31	1	2		

A Moon-day!

SHEEP: What was the first animal in space?

HORSE: The cow that jumped over the moon!

RIDDLE ME THIS ...

Q

I am a lion, but I don't roar. I'm found in the sky, but never on land. Who am I?

A The constellation Leo.

TONGUE TWISTER

SAY THIS FAST THREE TIMES:
Roaring rockets rise rapidly.

MELINA: I sent all your selfies to NASA.

ABE: Why?

MELINA: Because you're a star!

BIGGEST THINGS IN THE UNIVERSE

BIGGEST BLACK HOLE

TON 618

Giant black holes likely lurk in the center of every galaxy. But TON 618 may dwarf them all. Located in the constellation Aquila, it's a black hole the size of our solar system and has a mass—a measure of the stuff that makes up an object—of 66 billion suns.

BIGGEST GALAXY

IC 1101

Our own galaxy, the Milky Way, contains at least 100 billion stars. But as far as galaxies go, it's just average size. The largest galaxy, IC 1101, is 50 times bigger. It would take about six million years to fly through it at the speed of light.

BIGGEST OBJECT IN THE SOLAR SYSTEM

THE SUN

It appears as just a bright spot in the sky, but the sun is actually big—really big. It's by far the largest thing in our solar system, measuring about 865,000 miles (1.4 million km) across. If Earth were the size of a grape, the sun would be the size of a giant beach ball that's four feet (1.2 m) across!

BIGGEST FORCE

DARK MATTER AND DARK ENERGY

Everything that has ever been observed in space—all the planets, stars, dust, and everything else—makes up just 5 percent of the universe. The rest is made up of a mysterious, invisible substance called dark matter (25 percent) and a strange force called dark energy (70 percent).

BIGGEST STAR

UY SCUTI

If you thought our sun was big, take a peek at UY Scuti, the largest known star in the universe. If our sun were swapped with UY Scuti, UY Scuti would swallow up Mercury, Venus, Earth, and Mars, and its edges would extend past the orbit of Jupiter.

HOW MANY LIGHT-YEARS AWAY IS ...

Objects in space—such as planets, solar systems, and galaxies—are *really* far apart. Measuring their distance in miles would take some hugely gigantic numbers. So instead, we use light-years—that's the distance light travels in one Earth year. One light-year is about six trillion miles (10 trillion km). Here's how far away objects in space are from Earth, measured in the speed of light.

NOTE: DIAGRAM NOT TO SCALE

Earth

ONE LIGHT-MINUTE AWAY

ONE LIGHT-HOUR AWAY

The Moon
1.3 LIGHT-SECONDS

Mars
4.3 LIGHT-MINUTES

The Sun
8.3 LIGHT-MINUTES

Pluto
4.6 LIGHT-HOURS

Proxima Centauri
(our closest neighboring star)
4.3 LIGHT-YEARS

Polaris
(the North Star)
320 LIGHT-YEARS

Center of the Milky Way
26,000 LIGHT-YEARS

ONE LIGHT-YEAR AWAY

1,000 LIGHT-YEARS AWAY

100,000 LIGHT-YEARS AWAY

1 MILLION LIGHT-YEARS AWAY

1 BILLION LIGHT-YEARS AWAY

1 TRILLION LIGHT-YEARS AWAY

Andromeda
(our closest neighboring galaxy)
2.5 MILLION LIGHT-YEARS

GN-z11
(the oldest known galaxy)
13.4 BILLION LIGHT-YEARS

SCALE OF THE SOLAR SYSTEM

Have you ever stared at the faraway light of Mars or Venus in the night sky and wondered how big these planets really are? The size of the planets in the solar system can be hard to understand when you're standing on one of them. In this activity, you'll create a scale model of a solar system to learn just how big the planets are compared with each other.

YOU WILL NEED:
PAPER AND PENCIL
AT LEAST 5 POUNDS (2.3 KG) OF MODELING CLAY

STEP 1:

Write the name of each planet on a separate piece of paper and spread the papers out on a surface. This is where you will place each model planet.

STEP 2:

Using the modeling clay, make 10 balls of equal size. Take six of them and roll them together. This is Jupiter. Place it on the paper labeled with its name.

STEP 3:

Take another three balls and put them aside. This is part of Saturn. (You'll keep adding to Saturn later.)

STEP 4:

Take the clay that's left and divide it into 10 balls of the same size. Take five of them and add them to Saturn. Take another two and roll them together. This is Neptune. Take another two and roll them together to form Uranus.

STEP 5:

With the clay that's left, make 10 balls of the same size. Roll nine of them together and combine them with the rest of the clay for Saturn. Saturn is now complete.

STEP 6:

Take the clay that's left and divide it in half. One of the pieces is Earth.

STEP 7:

Then take the remaining piece and divide it into 10 same-size balls. Take nine of them and roll them together. This is Venus.

STEP 8:

For the final time, make 10 same-size balls out of the clay that's left. Use nine of them to create Mars. The clay that is left makes up Mercury.

STEP 9:

Your solar system is now complete! Compare the planets to each other. Do any of the sizes surprise you?

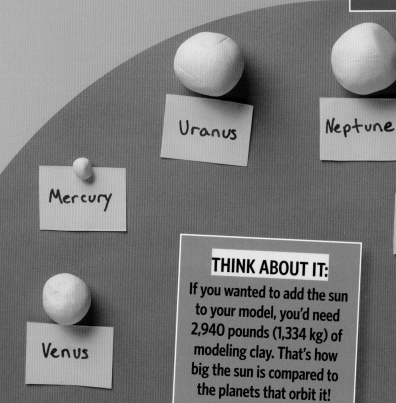

Uranus

Neptune

Mercury

Saturn

THINK ABOUT IT:

If you wanted to add the sun to your model, you'd need 2,940 pounds (1,334 kg) of modeling clay. That's how big the sun is compared to the planets that orbit it!

Venus

Earth

Mars

Jupiter

A NASA SPACE SUIT COSTS ABOUT
$250 MILLION
TO DESIGN AND MAKE.

A NASA SPACE SUIT WEIGHS ABOUT 280 POUNDS (127 KG) WITHOUT THE ASTRONAUT. (IT WEIGHS NOTHING IN SPACE.)

QUIZ TIME

ARE YOU AN ASTRONAUT EXPERT? FIND OUT HOW MUCH YOU KNOW ABOUT LIFE ON BOARD THE INTERNATIONAL SPACE STATION. CHECK YOUR ANSWERS ON THE BOTTOM OF PAGE 57.

TEST YOUR SPACE SMARTS

1 **What happens when you cry in space?**

a. Your tears stream down your cheeks.

b. Your tears puddle in your eyes.

c. Your tears float away.

d. Your body doesn't make tears in space.

2 **How do astronauts sleep?**

a. They go into a special gravity room.

b. They sleep sitting up, like you would in a car.

c. They crawl inside a hanging sleeping bag.

d. Astronauts don't need to sleep in space.

3 What happens if you have to scratch your nose on a space walk?

a. You just have to deal with it!

b. It's OK to take off your helmet, if you hold your breath.

c. Astronauts wear a special cream to keep themselves from itching.

d. There's a special itch strip in your helmet just for these occasions.

4 How do astronauts communicate with their friends and family?

a. They can't. There isn't cell phone coverage or internet access on the ISS.

b. They send emails and have video chats just like we do on Earth.

c. They make calls using their cell phones.

d. Astronauts' missions are top secret—they aren't allowed to communicate until they get home.

5 What do astronauts do for exercise in space?

a. They go to the space station gym.

b. They do yoga.

c. They go on daily space walks.

d. They work out to exercise videos.

3) d. It's true, astronauts can have a piece of Velcro or foam inside their helmets that they can rub their face against if they get an itch on a space walk!

2) c. When it's bedtime on the International Space Station, each astronaut goes to their sleep station, which is the size of a portable potty. Inside, they crawl into a sleeping bag, which is secured to the ceiling or a wall.

1) b. On the International Space Station, astronauts can form tears, but because there is less gravity there, the tears form a ball on their eyes. They don't stream down their cheeks or float away.

4) b. Astronauts leave their cell phones behind when they head to the space station, but they can still keep in touch with their families and friends. The ISS has internet access, which astronauts use for work and to check in with loved ones on Earth.

5) a. To combat the effects of microgravity, astronauts on board the space station need to exercise about two hours a day to prevent bone and muscle loss. So, they head to the gym—a designated area with a treadmill, an exercise bike, and a weight machine that the astronauts strap themselves into to work out.

ASTRONAUT RECORDS

MOST FAR-OUT DRIVE

DECEMBER 11–14, 1972

Are we there yet? Astronauts Eugene A. Cernan and Harrison H. "Jack" Schmitt drove a lunar rover nearly 20 miles (30.5 km) over three separate trips during the final manned moon mission to date. They collected 247 pounds (112 kg) of moon rock for scientists back on Earth to study.

LONGEST SPACE MISSION

JANUARY 1994–MARCH 1995

Talk about a long trip! Cosmonaut (that's a Russian astronaut) Valery Polyakov wanted to prove that a human could survive in space long enough for a future trip to Mars. He spent nearly 438 days on the Mir Space Station.

FIRST ALL-FEMALE SPACE WALK

OCTOBER 18, 2019

It was one giant leap for womankind! Astronauts Christina Koch and Jessica Meir spent more than seven hours floating in outer space, tethered to the International Space Station, as they worked to replace a battery component.

FASTEST FLIGHT

MAY 1969

Hold on to your helmets! On their way back from circling the moon, the astronauts who flew on NASA's Apollo 10 mission hit a blistering 24,791 miles an hour (39,897 km/h). That's more than 32 times the speed of sound!

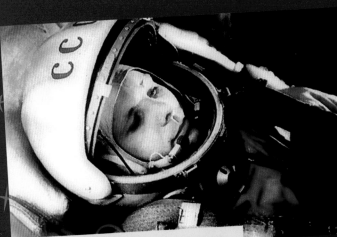

FIRST PERSON IN SPACE

APRIL 12, 1961

Humans left Earth for the first time when cosmonaut Yuri Gagarin blasted into orbit. After circling the planet, Gagarin managed to withstand g-forces eight times stronger than the pull of gravity, safely eject himself from his spacecraft, and parachute four miles (6.4 km) down to Earth.

OUT-THERE FACTS ABOUT NASA

A NASA scientist invented the Super Soaker.

Information gathered by the New Horizons spacecraft shows that Pluto probably has an ocean.

Astronaut John Young sneaked a **CORNED BEEF SANDWICH** onto the Gemini 3 mission in 1965.

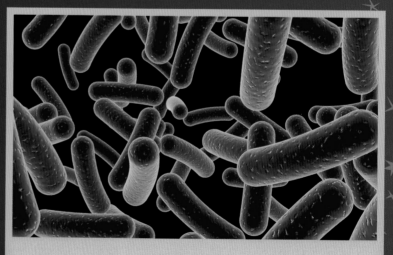

NASA has a planetary protection officer in charge of keeping Earth safe from alien microbes.

NASA SATELLITES TOM AND JERRY ARE NAMED AFTER THE CARTOON CAT AND MOUSE.

NASA space suits come with jet packs.

USING IMAGES FROM THE HUBBLE SPACE TELESCOPE, ASTRONOMERS HAVE FIGURED OUT THAT THE UNIVERSE IS ABOUT 14 BILLION YEARS OLD.

NASA's Kepler telescope discovered 2,662 planets outside our solar system.

NASA has SENT MANY ANIMALS TO SPACE, including fish, bees, and chimpanzees.

NASA research led to the invention of camera phones and ear thermometers.

NIGHT SKY
SCAVENGER HUNT

Look up! The night sky is full of tiny dots of light. But what are they? You can uncover the mysteries of the universe right from your backyard ... no telescope required!

YOU WILL NEED:

WHITE PENCIL OR CRAYON
BLACK CONSTRUCTION PAPER

STEP 1:

Pick a clear night with no clouds and head outside with the Cosmic Checklist (to the right).

Cosmic Checklist: How Many Objects Can You Find?

☐ **Constellations:** You might already know some of the constellations, like Orion and the Big Dipper. Which do you see tonight? What other shapes do you spot in the stars?

☐ **The Milky Way:** If you're lucky, you might see the Milky Way. It looks like a smudge of light that crosses the night sky.

☐ **The moon:** The moon shines because it reflects the sun's light. It appears to change shape because we see different amounts of it as the moon moves between Earth and the sun. What shape is it tonight?

☐ **Planets:** While stars twinkle, planets are dots of light that shine steadily. The five brightest planets (Mercury, Venus, Mars, Jupiter, and Saturn) are visible to the naked eye. They are visible for most of the year, but you won't see all of them on a single night.

☐ **Satellite:** Hundreds of satellites orbit Earth. They look like stars that move in a straight line and take several minutes to cross the sky.

☐ **Shooting star:** Actually a meteoroid that enters the atmosphere and burns up, this object will appear as a brief streak of light.

☐ **Sirius:** The brightest star in the night sky, Sirius is easy to see from the Northern Hemisphere during winter. To find it, locate Orion's belt. The belt's three stars point downward and to the left toward Sirius.

STEP 2:
Turn off all lights around you.

STEP 3:
Let your eyes adjust to the darkness. Be patient—this can take 20 to 45 minutes.

STEP 4:
Record your findings by drawing them on your black construction paper with the white pencil.

STEP 5:
Repeat the activity at different times of the year, and you'll see different objects as Earth orbits the sun.

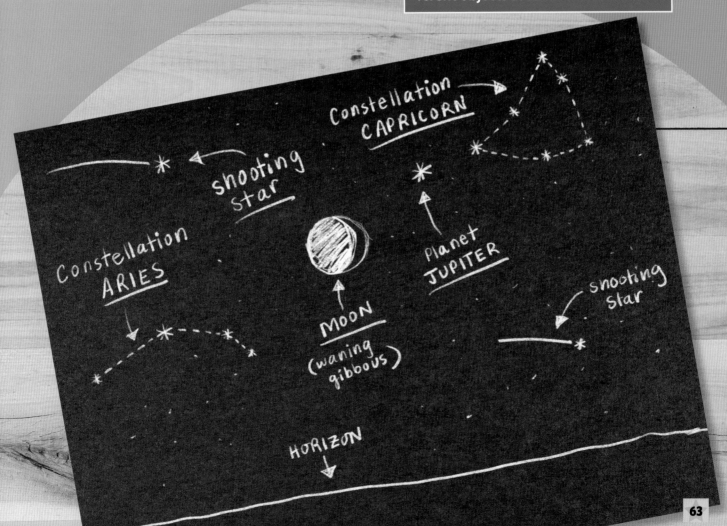

WATER ON MARS

MARS'S ICE CAPS CONTAIN ENOUGH WATER TO COVER THE ENTIRE PLANET WITH ABOUT 18 FEET (5.5 M) OF WATER.

Visit Mars today and you'd find a cold, dusty world. But billions of years ago, Mars looked very different. Scientists think it was a warm, wet world with rivers and oceans, much like Earth.

WATER WORLD

What happened to Mars? The red planet is smaller than Earth, with less gravity and a thinner atmosphere. Over billions of years, its water evaporated (turned from liquid into gas) until Mars dried out. But not all its water disappeared: Mars still has ice caps at its north and south poles. It also has frozen water beneath its surface. In 2015, astronomers discovered a slab of ice the size of the U.S. states of California and Texas combined between the equator and north pole. Some experts think Mars has liquid water, too. There is evidence of lakes deep beneath the planet's surface.

IN 2012, THE CURIOSITY ROVER ROLLED THROUGH AN ANCIENT STREAMBED ON MARS'S SURFACE.

ARE THERE MARTIANS?

Scientists are excited about these signs of water on Mars. That's because on Earth, everywhere there is water, there is life, too. Could tiny living things such as bacteria have once wiggled on the red planet—and could they still be hiding there today?

ARTWORK SHOWING WHAT MARS WOULD HAVE LOOKED LIKE ABOUT 3.5 BILLION YEARS AGO

SPACE SILLIES

Q What do you get when you cross a chicken with a Martian?

A An eggs-traterrestrial.

Q What's an astronaut's favorite snack food?

A Rocket chips.

Q What holds the sun up?

A Sun beams.

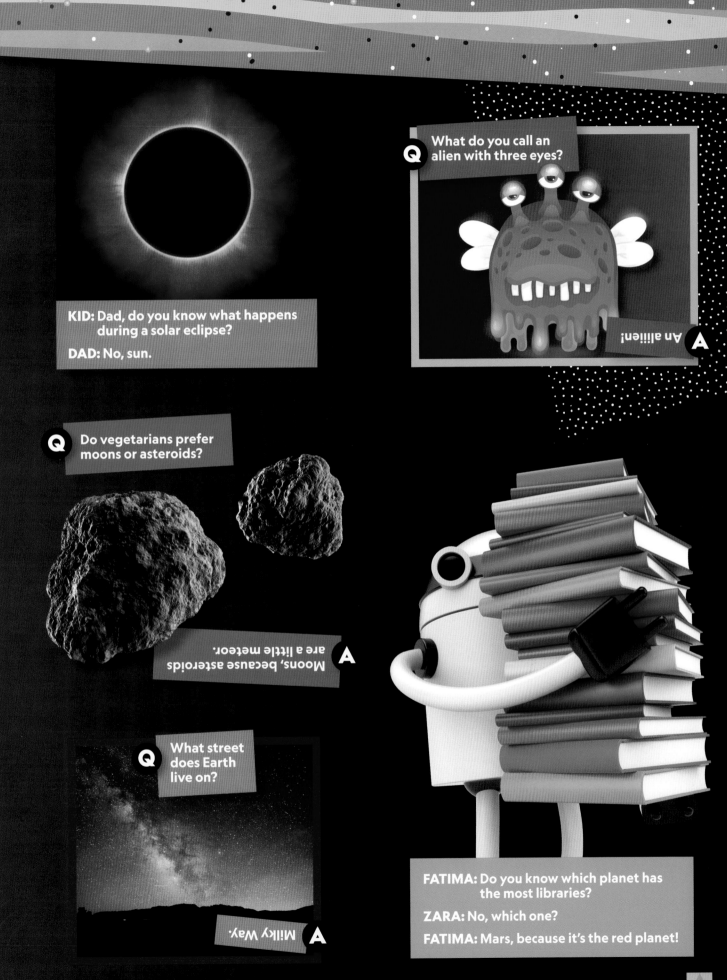

Q What do you call an alien with three eyes?

A An aliiiien!

KID: Dad, do you know what happens during a solar eclipse?

DAD: No, sun.

Q Do vegetarians prefer moons or asteroids?

A Moons, because asteroids are a little meteor.

Q What street does Earth live on?

A Milky Way.

FATIMA: Do you know which planet has the most libraries?

ZARA: No, which one?

FATIMA: Mars, because it's the red planet!

SPACE FOOD

When astronauts get hungry for a snack, they can't just tear open a bag of chips. Things get complicated when it comes to eating in space. Meals are carefully planned to make sure they are easy to prepare, and so that astronauts are getting all the nutrients they need to stay strong, healthy, and energetic. Everything eaten in space comes from Earth, so it has to be relatively lightweight, compact, and mostly nonperishable.

VELCRO IS ATTACHED TO FOOD POUCHES AND SILVERWARE TO KEEP THEM STUCK TO THE DINING TABLE SO THEY DON'T FLOAT AWAY DURING MEALS.

IN 1961, COSMONAUT YURI GAGARIN—THE FIRST PERSON TO ORBIT EARTH—ATE BEEF AND LIVER PASTE FROM A TUBE ON HIS JOURNEY.

BURPLESS BEVERAGES

If you tried to fill a glass with water in space, the water would simply float away. So astronauts sip theirs from a pouch with a straw. Lemonade and orange juice are also on the beverage menu, but not soda. When a soda can is opened in space, the bubbles don't rush to the top like they do on Earth. They stay in the can, which means astronauts take in more gas, causing more burps. That might sound like a good thing, but it turns out that in space, burps are a little painful and best avoided!

CRUMBY FOOD

Astronauts often eat packaged meals that come in special airtight pouches that can be heated in an oven. They assemble some of their own meals, too—like peanut butter and jelly sandwiches. But in space, bread is a major no-no! All those little crumbs left on your plate at the end of the meal would float away on the space station and could clog up vents or even get stuck in astronauts' eyes! Astronauts spread their PB and J on less crumbly tortillas instead.

ARE YOU AN EARTHLING OR AN ALIEN?

Are you more of a stargazer, or are your feet firmly planted on the ground? Take this quiz to find out if you are more of an alien or an Earthling.

1 Which would you rather dream about?
   a. swimming through a coral reef
   b. flying through the clouds

2 If you got to visit the International Space Station, which would you be most excited to do?
   a. eating the space food
   b. heading out for a space walk

3 You're headed to the carnival! Where do you go first?
   a. the game booths to try to win a stuffed animal
   b. the Tilt-a-Whirl ride

4 It's your birthday party! Which would you rather have for entertainment?

a. face painting and balloon animals

b. a bounce house

5 When looking through binoculars, which would you rather look at?

a. birds in a nest

b. the moon

IF YOU ANSWERED MOSTLY "A," YOU'RE MORE OF AN EARTHLING.

IF YOU ANSWERED MORE "B" YOU'RE MORE OF AN ALIEN.

IF THESE DESCRIPTIONS DON'T FIT YOU, THAT'S OK. THIS QUIZ IS JUST FOR FUN!

OUTER SPACE LOLs

KNOCK, KNOCK.

Who's there?
Astronaut.
Astronaut who?
Astro's not here, better come back later!

KID: Can we build an observatory in my room?
PARENT: Sorry, the cost would be astronomical.

Q What is an astronaut's favorite drink?

A Gravi-tea.

Q Why did the alien go to the doctor?

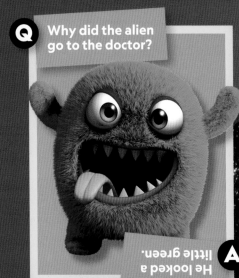

A He looked a little green.

Q What do astronauts turn on at night?

A Satel-lites.

RIDDLE ME THIS ...

Q I have been around for billions of years, but I am never more than a month old. What am I?

A The moon.

WHAT HAPPENS TO YOUR BODY IN SPACE?

Your body was made for a life on Earth—a place with gravity, oxygen, and an atmosphere that helps protect you from the sun's rays. Find out what happens to your body when you're in space and everything gets turned upside down.

SPINE
Without the pull of Earth's gravity, the human spine extends, making you a little bit taller! Once an astronaut returns to Earth, their height returns to normal.

BONES
Without gravity, bones lose minerals, causing the strength and thickness of bones to drop by more than one percent per month.

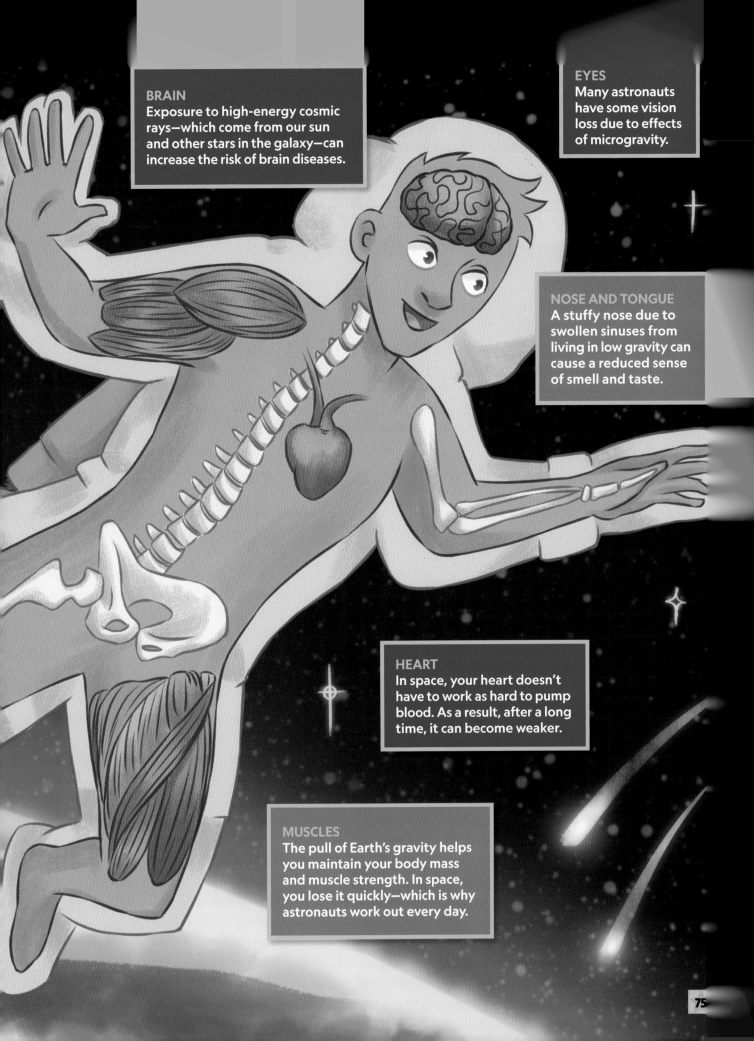

BRAIN
Exposure to high-energy cosmic rays—which come from our sun and other stars in the galaxy—can increase the risk of brain diseases.

EYES
Many astronauts have some vision loss due to effects of microgravity.

NOSE AND TONGUE
A stuffy nose due to swollen sinuses from living in low gravity can cause a reduced sense of smell and taste.

HEART
In space, your heart doesn't have to work as hard to pump blood. As a result, after a long time, it can become weaker.

MUSCLES
The pull of Earth's gravity helps you maintain your body mass and muscle strength. In space, you lose it quickly—which is why astronauts work out every day.

OVER THE MOON

The moon was probably born when **Theia,** a planet about the size of Mars, slammed into Earth, knocking loose debris that later **re-formed into the moon.**

The moon orbits Earth at about **2,300 miles an hour** (3,700 km/h).

THE MOON IS SLOWLY **MOVING AWAY** FROM EARTH.

Earth's tides are caused by the **moon's gravity** pulling on the water.

IN 2020, RESEARCHERS CONFIRMED FOR THE FIRST TIME THAT THERE IS **LIQUID WATER** ON THE MOON.

The moon's **huge craters** are the result of space rocks that **slammed** into it between 4.1 and 3.8 billion years ago.

THE MOON IS **BIGGER** THAN PLUTO.

THE MOON ISN'T ROUND; IT'S **EGG-SHAPED.**

The moon has **"moonquakes."**

Objects astronauts **have left on the moon** include a falcon feather, a photo of an astronaut's family, and **96 bags of human waste.**

MAKE A GALAXY MOBILE

A galaxy is a huge collection of gas and dust and billions of stars and planets, all held together by gravity. Our own galaxy, the Milky Way, is shaped like a giant spiral, but there are many galaxies besides ours—so many, we haven't counted them all yet! Here's how to make a mobile, so you can admire them up close.

WHAT YOU NEED:

BLACK CONSTRUCTION PAPER
METALLIC PENS
SCISSORS
TAPE MEASURE
CARDBOARD
GLUE
WHITE PENCIL
THREAD OR FISHING LINE
LARGE SEWING NEEDLE
BUTTON WITH FOUR HOLES

SAFETY NOTE!
ASK A GROWN-UP TO HELP YOU WITH THE SEWING AND CUTTING PARTS OF THIS ACTIVITY.

WHAT TO DO:

MAKE YOUR GALAXIES.

STEP 1:
Draw nine galaxies in the shapes of your choice on the paper, then decorate them with gel pens.

SPIRAL

BARRED SPIRAL

ELLIPTICAL

IRREGULAR

MAKE THE FRAME FOR YOUR MOBILE.

STEP 2:
Cut out a round circle of cardboard seven inches (18 cm) wide. Then cut out two pieces of black construction paper slightly larger than this circle, and glue them to each side of the cardboard to cover it.

STEP 3:

Next, make three pencil marks equally spaced around the edge of the circle, about one inch (2.5 cm) from the edge.

STEP 4:

Cut a length of thread about two feet (0.6 m) long. Thread the needle and tie a large knot in the end. Poke the needle through one of the pencil marks on your cardboard circle.

STEP 5:

Take the button and poke the needle up through one of its holes and down through another. Then poke the needle down through another mark on your circle, being sure the needle is going the opposite way it went in the last step.

STEP 6:

Unthread the needle and tie a large knot in the end of the thread.

STEP 7:

Now, cut another thread about three feet (1 m) long, rethread the needle, and tie a large knot in the end. Poke the needle up through the last pencil mark on the circle.

STEP 8:

Poke the needle up through one of the remaining buttonholes and then down through the last buttonhole. Unthread the needle and tie a loop in the end. You can use the loop to hang the mobile from the ceiling.

HANG THE GALAXIES FROM THE FRAME.

STEP 9:

Make nine evenly spaced marks on the bottom side of your mobile frame. Cut a length of thread and tie a knot in the end. Then push the needle through the center of a galaxy. Next, push it through one of the marks on the circle and tie a knot in the end.

STEP 10:

Repeat with the remaining galaxies. Be sure to hang them at different heights, so they don't hit each other.

STEP 11:

Finally, hang your galaxy mobile from the ceiling. Look at all those glittering galaxies!

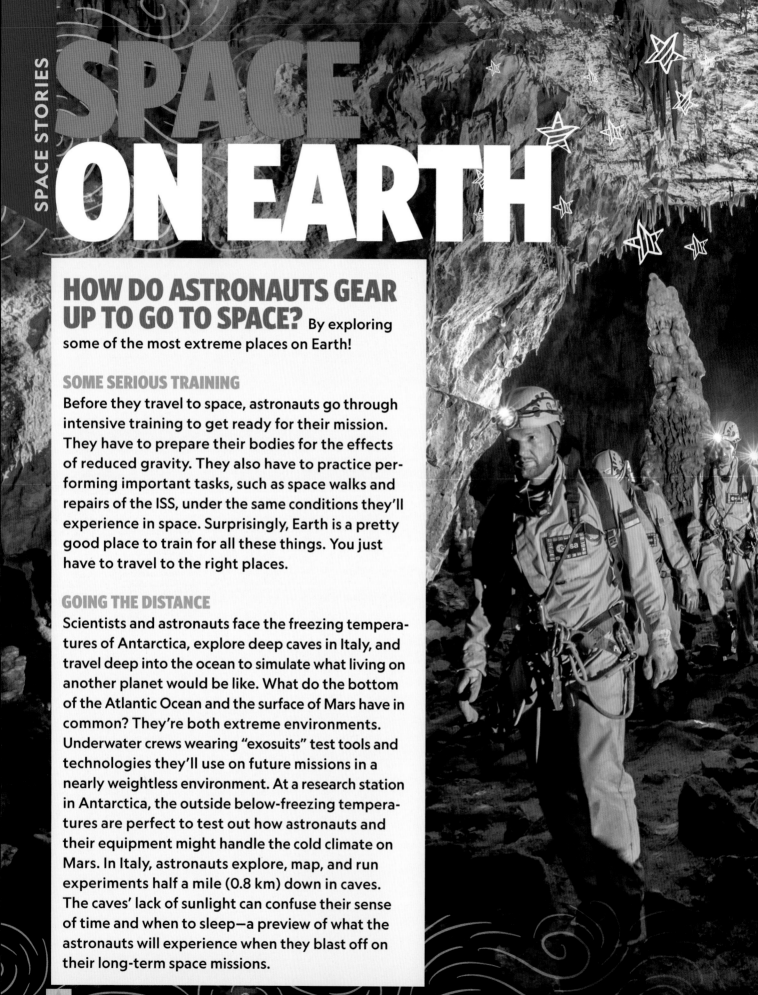

SPACE ON EARTH

HOW DO ASTRONAUTS GEAR UP TO GO TO SPACE? By exploring some of the most extreme places on Earth!

SOME SERIOUS TRAINING

Before they travel to space, astronauts go through intensive training to get ready for their mission. They have to prepare their bodies for the effects of reduced gravity. They also have to practice performing important tasks, such as space walks and repairs of the ISS, under the same conditions they'll experience in space. Surprisingly, Earth is a pretty good place to train for all these things. You just have to travel to the right places.

GOING THE DISTANCE

Scientists and astronauts face the freezing temperatures of Antarctica, explore deep caves in Italy, and travel deep into the ocean to simulate what living on another planet would be like. What do the bottom of the Atlantic Ocean and the surface of Mars have in common? They're both extreme environments. Underwater crews wearing "exosuits" test tools and technologies they'll use on future missions in a nearly weightless environment. At a research station in Antarctica, the outside below-freezing temperatures are perfect to test out how astronauts and their equipment might handle the cold climate on Mars. In Italy, astronauts explore, map, and run experiments half a mile (0.8 km) down in caves. The caves' lack of sunlight can confuse their sense of time and when to sleep—a preview of what the astronauts will experience when they blast off on their long-term space missions.

NASA ASTRONAUTS TRAIN IN A 6.2-MILLION-GALLON (23.5-MILLION-L) INDOOR SWIMMING POOL IN HOUSTON, TEXAS, U.S.A.

ASTRONAUTS WHO TRAIN IN CAVES ARE CALLED CAVENAUTS.

TEMPERATURES AT THE ANTARCTICA RESEARCH STATION WHERE ASTRONAUTS TRAIN GET AS LOW AS MINUS 112°F (-80°C)!

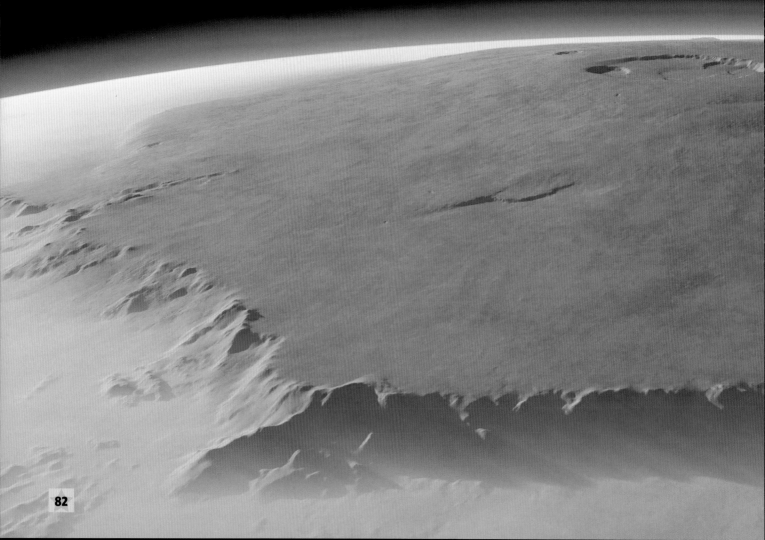

OLYMPUS MONS, THE LARGEST VOLCANO IN THE SOLAR SYSTEM, IS LOCATED ON MARS.

OLYMPUS MONS IS ABOUT THREE TIMES THE HEIGHT OF MOUNT EVEREST, **THE HIGHEST MOUNTAIN ON EARTH.**

MISSION TO EUROPA

ABOUT 400 MILLION MILES (640 MILLION KM) AWAY FROM EARTH floats Jupiter's moon Europa. It's covered with ice and crisscrossed with long, reddish cracks. But scientists believe that miles beneath that icy surface is an enormous ocean. And they think that ocean may be the most promising place to find life in our solar system.

GETTING THERE

NASA hopes to launch a spacecraft to Europa to take a closer look. Called Europa Clipper, it will orbit Jupiter and make about 40 close flybys of the moon to get information about its ocean. Europa Clipper will also scout landing sites for a potential future mission to land a craft on Europa's surface, drill through its ice, and plunge into its waters to find out if there's anything—or anyone—swimming there.

EUROPA'S ICY SURFACE MAY GLOW IN THE DARK.

EUROPA MAY HAVE GIANT GEYSERS THAT SPRAY WATER HIGH INTO ITS SKY.

THE ICE THAT COVERS EUROPA COULD BE UP TO 105 MILES (170 KM) THICK.

NAME THAT ALL-STAR ASTRONAUT

CAN YOU MATCH THE FAMOUS ASTRONAUTS TO THEIR OUT-OF-THIS-WORLD ACCOMPLISHMENTS? FIND THE ANSWERS AT THE BOTTOM OF PAGE 87.

1

Date of birth: February 15, 1964
Space missions: STS-122, STS-129 (space shuttle missions)
Famous for: The only person drafted into the NFL to have flown in space
Famous quote: "I didn't see any borders. I saw this fragile blue planet that we are all in charge of ensuring that we keep it sustained."

2

Date of birth: May 26, 1951
Space missions: STS-7, STS-41-G (space shuttle missions)
Famous for: The first American woman in space, in 1983
Famous quote: "I was always very interested in science, and I knew that for me, science was a better long-term career than tennis."

ASTRONAUTS AND COSMONAUTS

NEIL ARMSTRONG

YURI GAGARIN

VALENTINA TERESHKOVA

3

Date of birth: February 21, 1964

Space missions: STS-103, STS-118 (space shuttle missions); Expedition 25/26, Expedition 43/44/45/46 (ISS)

Famous for: Spending nearly one year on board the International Space Station

Famous quote: "I miss cooking. I miss chopping fresh food, the smell vegetables give up when you first slice into them."

4

Date of birth: March 6, 1937

Space missions: Vostok 6

Famous for: First woman in space; orbited Earth 48 times in 1963

Famous quote: "Once you've been in space, you appreciate how small and fragile the Earth is."

5

Date of birth: March 9, 1934

Space missions: Vostok 1

Famous for: First human to orbit Earth

Famous quote: "I see Earth! It is so beautiful!"

6

Date of birth: August 5, 1930

Space missions: Apollo 11, Gemini 8

Famous for: The first person to walk on the moon

Famous quote: "That's one small step for a man, one giant leap for mankind."

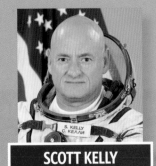

SCOTT KELLY

LELAND MELVIN

SALLY RIDE

ANSWERS: 1. Leland Melvin; 2. Sally Ride; 3. Scott Kelly; 4. Valentina Tereshkova; 5. Yuri Gagarin; 6. Neil Armstrong

87

ROCKING IT

EVERY DAY, MORE THAN 100 TONS (91 T) OF SPACE ROCK STRIKE EARTH.

Asteroids are chunks of rock left over from when our solar system formed about **4.6 billion years ago.**

In 2001, NASA flight controllers **landed a spacecraft on an asteroid** for the first time.

A **METEORITE** IS A METEOR THAT LANDS ON EARTH.

Comets are sometimes called **"dirty snowballs"** because they are often made mostly of frozen water with bits of rock inside.

A **METEOR SHOWER** HAPPENS WHEN EARTH PASSES THROUGH THE TRAIL OF DUST FROM AN ASTEROID OR COMET.

Ceres was considered an asteroid until it was reclassified as a **dwarf planet** in 2006.

Ancients Chinese astronomers kept records of **comets** for centuries. Modern astronomers still use the information they gathered.

ASTEROIDS CAN HAVE THEIR OWN MOONS.

THE **BIGGEST METEORITE** EVER DISCOVERED WEIGHS 66 TONS (60 T), OR THE WEIGHT OF ABOUT NINE LARGE AFRICAN **ELEPHANTS.**

OUTER SPACE LOLs

Q What do astronauts drink on the moon?

A Crater-ade.

Q What do you get when you cross a Martian with a kangaroo?

A A Mars-upial.

Q Where do planets and stars go to school?

A The universe-ity.

90

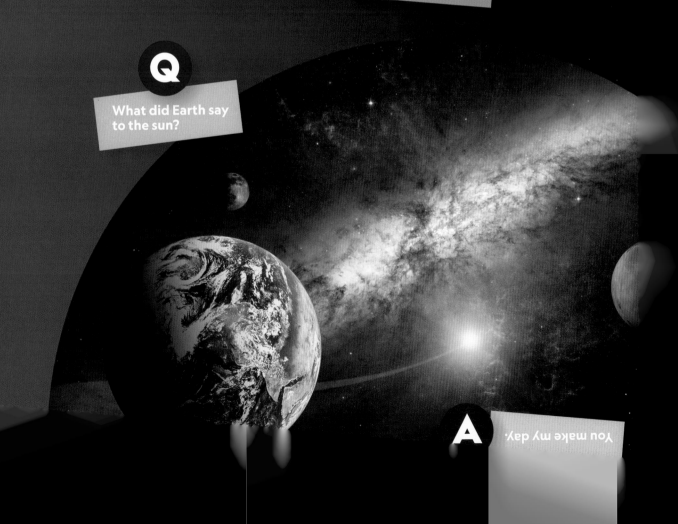

MOST FAR-OUT THINGS IN SPACE

FARTHEST KNOWN PLANET

OGLE-TR-56B

Discovered in 2002, planet OGLE-TR-56b is 922 light-years away, making it the most distant planet discovered so far. Its surface is about 3100°F (1704°C)—so hot it may rain liquid iron there.

FARTHEST OBJECT YOU CAN SEE WITH THE NAKED EYE

THE ANDROMEDA GALAXY

The Andromeda galaxy, 2.5 million light-years away, is the most distant object possible to spot without a telescope. Since a light-year is the distance light travels in a year, that means that when you look at Andromeda, you're actually seeing it as it was 2.5 million years ago.

FARTHEST HUMAN-MADE OBJECT

VOYAGER 1

NASA spacecraft Voyager 1 was launched in 1977 to explore the outer planets in the solar system. After accomplishing that mission, it exited the solar system and is now more than 14 billion miles (22.5 billion km) from planet Earth.

FARTHEST STAR

ICARUS

A bright blue star named Icarus is the farthest star spotted so far. It's nine billion light-years from Earth, more than halfway across the known universe.

FARTHEST OBJECT IN THE SOLAR SYSTEM

"FAROUT"

In 2018, astronomers spotted an object orbiting at more than 100 times the distance from Earth to the sun—so far away, scientists estimate it would take more than 1,000 years to complete a trip. Scientists think it's a round, pinkish-colored dwarf planet. Its nickname? "Farout."

93

LIVING IN SPACE

Astronauts grow up to **3 percent taller** while living in space because of the **lack of gravity.**

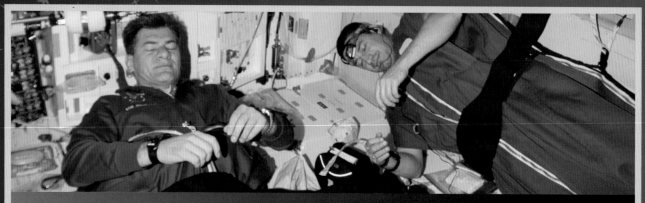

ASTRONAUTS HAVE TO STRAP THEIR **SLEEPING BAGS** TO THE WALL.

Astronauts on a space walk can get **"the bends,"** a sickness that also affects scuba divers and can cause **dizziness, headache, and trouble thinking clearly.**

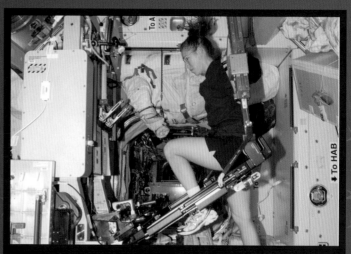

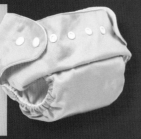

ASTRONAUTS WEAR DIAPERS ON SPACE WALKS.

On the International Space Station, a special system **collects moisture** from astronauts' breath, sweat, and even their pee, and **recycles it for drinking water.**

IN 2015, ASTRONAUTS ATE
THE FIRST SPACE SALAD
MADE WITH LETTUCE GROWN ON THE
INTERNATIONAL SPACE STATION.

When they come back to Earth, astronauts often **drop objects.** They're used to **zero gravity** keeping things afloat!

ASTRONAUTS'
SENSE OF TASTE
WEAKENS IN SPACE. THEY GO THROUGH A LOT OF **HOT SAUCE!**

ASTRONAUTS USE
NO-RINSE SHAMPOO
TO WASH THEIR HAIR IN SPACE.

Salt and pepper
have to be in
liquid form
in space, so the particles don't float around.

ASTRONAUTS ON THE INTERNATIONAL SPACE STATION SEE A
SUNRISE EVERY 90 MINUTES.

A PLANET WITH TWO SUNS

Love sunsets? Then you might be right at home on Kepler-16b. This exoplanet, located 245 light-years from Earth, orbits double suns. That means if you could visit, you'd watch two sunsets—and two sunrises—every day!

FAR-OUT FIND

When Kepler-16b was first discovered, in 2011, it was the only planet orbiting two suns ever found. Since then, astronomers have discovered many more. Technically called "circumbinary" planets, they're often nicknamed "Tatooine" planets after the dusty, twin-sunned world in *Star Wars*.

TWICE AS NICE

Circumbinary planets aren't as unusual as they may sound. Solar systems with twin suns are more common than solar systems with a single sun, like ours. And some scientists believe they could be ideal places to host alien life. One thing is for sure—anything living on one of these planets has a spectacular view!

NASA's Jet Propulsion Laboratory produced vintage-style travel posters for some newly discovered exoplanets, including Kepler-16b.

IF YOU WERE STANDING ON A DOUBLE-SUN PLANET, YOU'D HAVE TWO SHADOWS.

AN ILLUSTRATION SHOWING THE TWO SUNS FROM ONE OF THE HYPOTHETICAL MOONS OF KEPLER-16B

THE GOLDEN RECORDS

More than 40 years ago, two probes called Voyager 1 and 2 were launched into space, each carrying a "Golden Record." The identical records are 12-inch (31-cm) gold-plated copper disks surrounded by an aluminum case. A cartridge and needle were included to play each record, along with instructions, written in symbols. The records, which are now beyond our solar system in interstellar space, are a time capsule of sorts. If found by intelligent extraterrestrial life, they will reveal information about life on Earth—and where to find us. Here is some of what they contain.

A committee chaired by cosmologist and author Carl Sagan (above right) selected the contents of the Golden Record. Author Ann Druyan (above left) was the project's creative director.

The aluminum cover is engraved with a galactic map that shows how to find Earth.

Photographs, 115 in total, including
- athletes of the time
- people eating and drinking
- buildings, including the Taj Mahal and the Golden Gate Bridge
- animals, including crocodiles
- agriculture and farming

Greetings in 55 languages, including Arabic, Cantonese, Nepali, and English

Twelve minutes of sounds, including ocean waves, thunder, whales, crickets, laughter, a train, and a heartbeat

Ninety minutes of music, including classical music, like the works of Bach and Mozart; Aboriginal songs from Australia; and Azerbaijani bagpipes

SPACE JUNK!

TRASH IS EVERYWHERE: ON LAND, IN THE SEA—EVEN IN SPACE!

There are 23,000 human-made objects four inches (10 cm) or larger orbiting Earth, and millions more smaller ones zipping around it, too. How did they get there?

STRAY SATELLITES

As soon as people started exploring space, they left objects behind. This all started in 1957, when the first satellite, Sputnik I, was launched. Some 10,000 satellites have been launched into low-orbit space since then. Although most of them are broken or have stopped working, they're still up there, cruising at nearly 18,000 miles an hour (29,000 km/h) in constant orbit. The more cluttered low-orbit space gets, the more likely bits and pieces are going to crash into working satellites, or even the International Space Station (ISS). Some people have proposed using a giant magnet to clean up the junk. Others suggest a type of net to scoop up the trash and bring it into Earth's atmosphere, where it will burn up.

WASTE IN SPACE

But satellites aren't the only items left behind. Astronauts have left human-made objects on the moon—like exploration buggies, golf balls, and a photograph—which are considered space junk. They have also accidentally dropped trash into space when out on space walks, including a camera, a spatula, a glove, and a pair of pliers. Other human-made objects have ventured beyond our solar system, like the Voyager 1 and Voyager 2 probes launched in the 1970s. It just goes to show that one person's (space) junk is another person's scientific treasure!

THIS DEBRIS SHIELD WAS JETTISONED FROM THE ISS.

BETWEEN 200 AND 400 PIECES OF SPACE JUNK ENTER EARTH'S ATMOSPHERE EACH YEAR.

THE NANORACKS-REMOVE DEBRIS SATELLITE AIMS TO ADDRESS THE PROBLEM BY CAPTURING SPACE JUNK ORBITING EARTH.

SPACE SILLIES

KNOCK, KNOCK.

Who's there?
Lunar.
Lunar who?
Lunar or later these jokes are going to get better!

Q Why did the astronaut bring paint and paper on his trip?

A So he could do space crafts.

Q How does the man in the moon get his hair cut?

A Eclipse it!

Q What do you call a pecan on a spaceship?

A An astro-nut!

ALEX: I'm totally obsessed with the moon.

PETER: Maybe it's just a phase.

MILES: I checked out a book on antigravity.

BRIANNA: How is it?

MILES: I can't put it down.

RIDDLE ME THIS ...

Q

You see through me, but I can see farther than you can. What am I?

MAYA: I'm so disappointed.

JUAN: How come?

MAYA: I keep pressing the space bar on my computer, but I'm still here on Earth.

A A telescope.

BRILLIANT FACTS ABOUT GALAXIES

When you look up at the **night sky,** all the stars you can see are part of the **Milky Way galaxy.**

OUR GALAXY, **THE MILKY WAY,** BEGAN FORMING MORE THAN **13 BILLION YEARS AGO.**

THE MOST COMMON GALAXY SHAPE IS A **SPIRAL.**

Galaxies are moving **farther apart** as the universe **expands.**

Most galaxies are **dwarf galaxies,** or galaxies smaller than one-tenth the size of the Milky Way.

IN ABOUT FOUR BILLION YEARS, THE MILKY WAY WILL COLLIDE WITH ITS NEIGHBOR, THE ANDROMEDA GALAXY.

The Milky Way rotates at about 570,000 miles an hour (917,000 km/h).

THE WORD "GALAXY" COMES FROM THE GREEK WORD FOR "MILK."

Until 1924, many astronomers thought that the Milky Way was the only galaxy in space.

THE SOMBRERO GALAXY HAS A LARGE BULGE IN THE CENTER SURROUNDED BY A RING OF DUST, RESEMBLING THE MEXICAN HAT IT'S NAMED AFTER.

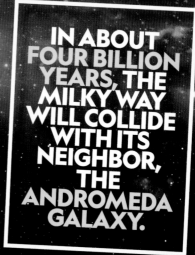

SEEN FROM SPACE

THE GRAND CANYON

Most of Earth looks like a swirl of blue, green, and white from space, but some objects—both human-made and natural—are so big that astronauts can spot them from 250 miles (400 km) up in the International Space Station.

ASTRONAUTS GET A BIRD'S-EYE VIEW OF ERUPTING VOLCANOES, INCLUDING RAIKOKE, A REMOTE VOLCANO IN THE NORTH PACIFIC OCEAN, WHICH THEY PHOTOGRAPHED IN 2019.

ASIA
ARCTIC OCEAN
EUROPE
The River Thames Paris
NORTH AMERICA
AFRICA
Grand Canyon
ATLANTIC OCEAN
PACIFIC OCEAN
Amazon River
SOUTH AMERICA

HURRICANES

THE FIRST IMAGE OF EARTH TAKEN FROM BEYOND THE ATMOSPHERE WAS TAKEN FROM A ROCKET IN 1946.

THE AMAZON RIVER

THE RIVER THAMES

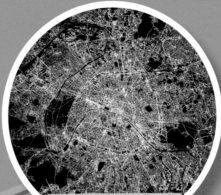

PARIS [LIT UP AT NIGHT]

THE HIMALAYAN MOUNTAINS

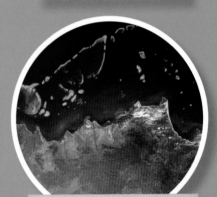

AUSTRALIA'S GREAT BARRIER REEF

NORTH AMERICA

ARCTIC OCEAN

EUROPE

The Pyramids at Giza

ASIA

AFRICA

Artificial palm-shaped islands

The Himalaya

PACIFIC OCEAN

INDIAN OCEAN

Great Barrier Reef

THE PYRAMIDS AT GIZA

HUMAN-MADE PALM-SHAPED ISLANDS IN THE UNITED ARAB EMIRATES

SPOOKY SPACE SCRAMBLE

There are no tricks here. These space objects with Halloween-like names are the real deal! Unscramble the spooky names, then check your answers at the bottom of page 109.

1 VAEMPRI star

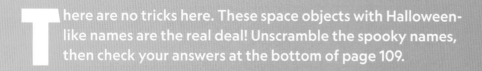

2 FNESTNIKENRA galaxy

3 TCWHI DHAE
Nebula

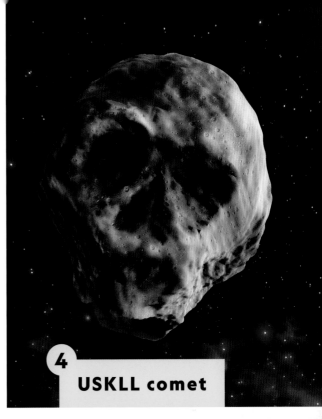

4 USKLL comet

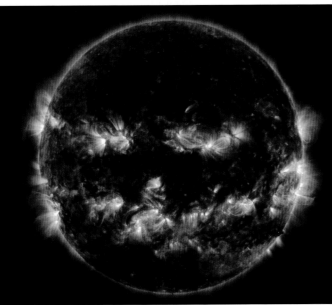

5 JCKA O
NTANELR sun

6 OGHST
galaxy

THE WATERFALL

NEBULA

IS ONE OF THE MOST

MYSTERIOUS OBJECTS

DISCOVERED IN THE UNIVERSE.

NO ONE KNOWS

HOW IT FORMED.

THE "WATERFALL" IS ABOUT
10 LIGHT-YEARS LONG.

SPACE VOLCANOES

VOLCANOES AREN'T JUST AN EARTH THING—they're found on planets and moons throughout our solar system. But there are only a few places we know of that have volcanoes that are currently active. Forty years ago, NASA got its first look at an erupting volcano on Io, one of Jupiter's moons. Volcanoes there released plumes of gas and melted rock up to 300 miles (480 km) upward, which was high enough for NASA spacecraft to catch a glimpse.

CRYOVOLCANOES

Neptune's moon Triton and Saturn's moon Enceladus (en-SAH-la-duss) have even more extreme volcanoes. Instead of erupting hot lava, these volcanoes erupt geysers of nitrogen gas and water. And instead of bright orange flows, there are flows of ammonia and water.

UNDERCOVER, MASSIVE, AND NEARBY VOLCANOES

Venus has more volcanoes than any other place in the solar system, but it's unclear if any of the volcanoes are active right now. Scientists can't see through Venus's atmosphere to find out, but they can get a peek at what's underneath its clouds using radar. They do know that the volcanoes there have erupted flows of lava, which can be seen on the surface by the radar. A volcanic eruption has never been seen on Mars, but it is home to the largest volcano in our solar system—Olympus Mons, which is about the size of the U.S. state of Arizona. Even Earth's moon had volcanoes! Lava flows on the moon's surface are telltale signs that it once had volcanic activity—but long before any human could have seen it through a telescope. Volcanic activity on the moon stopped about 100 million years ago.

VOLCANOES ON THE MOON MAY HAVE ERUPTED AT THE SAME TIME THERE WERE DINO-SAURS ON EARTH.

PANCAKE VOLCANOES, FOUND ON VENUS, ARE FLAT-TOPPED AND WIDE.

OUTER SPACE LOLs

KNOCK, KNOCK.

Who's there?
Saturn.
Saturn who?
I sat on my phone, otherwise I would have just called!

Q Why didn't the sun go to college?

A It already had a million degrees.

Q What did the astronaut say to mission control after she crash-landed on the moon?

A She Apollo-gized.

TONGUE TWISTER

TRY SAYING THIS FAST THREE TIMES:
Poor Pluto was too petite to compete.

DOMINIC: How did the snail travel to the moon?

ALEXANDRIA: How?

DOMINIC: It traveled at a snail's space.

ZOE: Why is it hard for astronauts to play golf in space?

SETH: I don't know, why?

ZOE: There are a lot of black holes.

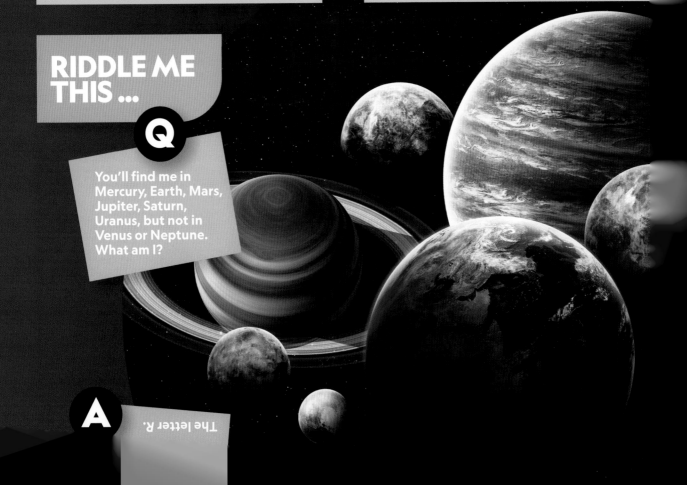

RIDDLE ME THIS ...

Q

You'll find me in Mercury, Earth, Mars, Jupiter, Saturn, Uranus, but not in Venus or Neptune. What am I?

A The letter R.

GUESS THAT MYSTERY PLANET

Read the clues, write down your guesses, then check your answers at the bottom of the page!

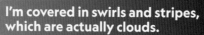

1

I'M KNOWN FOR MY SIZE.

I'm covered in swirls and stripes, which are actually clouds.

I have a storm bigger than Earth that's been hanging around for hundreds of years.

I'm orbited by dozens of moons.

ANSWERS: 1. Jupiter, 2. Uranus, 3. Mercury, 4. Mars

116

I'M KNOWN AS AN ICE GIANT.

My nickname is "sideways planet" because I rotate on my side.

My 27 moons are named after characters in poems and plays.

I have rings.

2

3

I'M ONLY A LITTLE LARGER THAN EARTH'S MOON.

I'm a rocky planet with lots of craters.

I don't have any moons or rings.

I am the second hottest planet.

4

EARTH IS ALMOST TWICE AS WIDE AS ME.

I have ice caps, canyons, and volcanoes.

I have two moons, but no rings.

I am considered a cold desert planet.

BRIGHT FACTS ABOUT STARS

On a clear night, in very dark areas of Earth, you can see more than **4,500 stars** with the naked eye.

OUR SUN IS A **DWARF STAR**—EVEN THOUGH IT'S NEARLY **865,000 MILES** (1.4 MILLION KM) ACROSS!

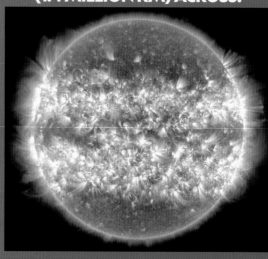

STARS DON'T ACTUALLY **TWINKLE**—IT'S AN EFFECT OF HOW THEIR LIGHT TRAVELS THROUGH **EARTH'S ATMOSPHERE.**

STARS ARE ABOUT 73 PERCENT **HYDROGEN,** 25 PERCENT HELIUM, AND 2 PERCENT OTHER **ELEMENTS.**

Proxima Centauri, the closest star to the sun, is still so far away from our planet that it takes its light more than **four years** to travel to Earth.

ABOUT **275 MILLION** NEW STARS ARE BORN OR DIE **EVERY DAY** IN THE KNOWN UNIVERSE.

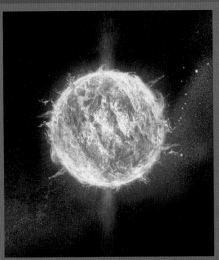

Neutron stars contain more matter than our sun but are smaller than a city.

THE LEAST **MASSIVE STARS** LIVE THE LONGEST.

THE OLDEST KNOWN **STAR CHART,** FROM ANCIENT EGYPT, DATES BACK TO **1534** B.C.

Most stars are **binary,** or a pair of double stars that **orbit together.**

A STAR CAN BE RED, BLUE, YELLOW, OR WHITE, DEPENDING ON ITS **TEMPERATURE.**

QUIZ TIME

CONGRATULATIONS! BY NOW YOU'RE A REAL SPACE EXPERT! TAKE THIS QUIZ TO FIND OUT HOW MUCH YOU REMEMBER ABOUT THE FACTS YOU LEARNED IN THIS BOOK. CHECK YOUR ANSWERS ON THE BOTTOM OF PAGE 121.

1 How long can an astronaut's footprints on the moon last?

    a. up to a year

    b. 1,000 years

    c. one million years

    d. They blow away almost immediately.

3 Which planet in our solar system has the hottest temperatures?

    a. Mercury

    b. Mars

    c. Venus

    d. Jupiter

2 How fast does our solar system move around the Milky Way?

    a. 120,000 miles an hour (193,100 km/h)

    b. 515,000 miles an hour (829,000 km/h)

    c. 91 million miles an hour (146,450,000 km/h)

    d. Trick question! Our solar system doesn't move.

4 Which planet is home to Olympus Mons, the largest volcano in our solar system?

    a. Mars

    b. Earth

    c. Jupiter

    d. Uranus

5 How big is Jupiter?

    a. about as big as the sun

    b. five times as big as Earth

    c. twice as massive as all the other planets combined

    d. twice the size of Saturn

6 **What is Neptune known for?**

a. its large waves

b. its many moons

c. its canyons

d. its strong winds

11 **True or False**

If you were to pour a glass of water on Mars, it would instantly freeze.

7 **True or False**

Soda is the most popular beverage on the International Space Station.

12 **What space object is nicknamed a "dirty snowball"?**

a. a satellite that reenters Earth's atmosphere

b. a comet, because it's made of frozen water with rocks inside

c. white moon rock brought back from the Apollo missions

d. waste released from the International Space Station

8 **True or False**

You get taller in space.

9 **How many planets are thought to be in the Milky Way?**

a. 100,000

b. 100 million

c. 100 billion

d. 100 trillion

10 **True or False**

Scientists discovered a planet that is made partly of diamond.

FIND OUT MORE

Want to explore more of the universe? Ask a grown-up to help you check out these books and online resources. And if you're looking for places to visit that will transport you to outer space, we've got you covered with a list of suggestions.

BOOKS

National Geographic Kids Everything Space: Blast Off for a Universe of Photos, Facts, and Fun! by Helaine Becker

National Geographic Kids Space Encyclopedia: A Tour of Our Solar System and Beyond by David A. Aguilar

National Geographic Little Kids First Big Book of Space by Catherine D. Hughes

PLACES TO GO

Adler Planetarium (Chicago, Illinois)

American Museum of Natural History Hayden Planetarium (New York City)

Kennedy Space Center (Florida)

San Diego Air and Space Museum (California)

Smithsonian National Air and Space Museum (Washington, D.C.)

Earth

ONLINE RESOURCES

Britannica Kids: Space Exploration

NASA Jet Propulsion Laboratory

NASA Space Place

NASA StarChild

National Geographic: Our Solar System

National Geographic Kids: Passport to Space

Nine Planets

Smithsonian National Air and Space Museum: Exploring the Planets

Space Camp

Lake of ice on Mars

INDEX

CREDITS